BENNY'S NEW FRIEND

Created by **Gertrude Chandler Warner**

Illustrated by **Daniel Mark Duffy**

SCHOLASTIC INC.

New York Toronto London Auckland Sydney

ISBN 0-590-10040-8

Copyright © 1998 by Albert Whitman & Company.
All rights reserved. Published by Scholastic Inc.,
555 Broadway, New York, NY 10012,
by arrangement with Albert Whitman & Company.
THE BOXCAR CHILDREN is a registered trademark of Albert Whitman
& Company. THE ADVENTURES OF BENNY AND WATCH
is a trademark of Albert Whitman & Company.
SCHOLASTIC and associated logos are trademarks
and/or registered trademarks of Scholastic Inc.

12 11 10 9 8 7 6 5 4 3 2 1   8 9/9 0 1 2/0

Printed in the U.S.A.   23

First Scholastic printing, February 1998

The Boxcar Children

Henry, Jessie, Violet, and Benny Alden are
orphans. They are supposed to live with their
grandfather, but they have heard that he is mean.
So the children run away and live in an old red
boxcar. They find a dog, and Benny names him
Watch.

When Grandfather finds them, the children
see that he is not mean at all. They happily go to
live with him. And, as a surprise, Grandfather
brings the boxcar along!

The Alden family sat around the dinner table. Watch, their dog, sat under the table waiting for food to drop.

Henry said, "Benny, I hear a kid who's just your age moved in down the road."

"Wow," Benny said. "I'd like a new friend."

The next morning, Benny ran outside. He yelled to Jessie, "I'm going to see the new kid." He hopped on his bike. Watch ran alongside him.

When Benny reached the end of the road he saw a child playing with a ball. Benny could only see the back of the boy. He heard a loud THWACK as the ball was caught.

The boy turned around. On the front
of his sweatshirt was the name BETH.
"You're a *girl*!" Benny shouted.

"So," Beth said. "What's wrong with *that*?"
"Nothing, I guess," Benny said, frowning.
"Want to play catch?" Beth asked. "Here's a mitt."
Benny put on the mitt. "I throw a pretty fast ball," he said. "Maybe too fast for you."

Beth threw the ball to Benny.
THWACK!
Benny was surprised. Beth
could throw fast, too!
Then something awful happened.
When Benny threw the ball back
to Beth, it was wide. Very wide!
Watch chased the ball and took it
to Beth.

She threw to Benny again. The
ball hit his mitt with a loud THWACK.
But when it was Benny's turn, the
ball went wide again. Very wide!
Watch had to chase it again.

Benny threw the mitt down. "I have to go home for lunch," he said.

Beth frowned. "But it's only ten-thirty."

Benny looked away. "Well, sometimes we eat lunch early."

He got on his bike and rode
home. Watch was close behind.

That night, Henry asked, "How was the new kid?"

"He was a *girl!*" Benny said. "I don't like to play with girls."

Jessie laughed. "Well, Violet and
I are girls. You play with us."

Benny said, "You're not really *girls*.
You're just sisters."

Everyone laughed.

The next day, Benny decided to go into
the woods behind his house to pick berries.
Jessie gave him a pail and said, "Don't go too far."

The woods were cool and dark. Benny picked the berries from the bushes. Watch ate all the ones that fell to the ground. Benny began to run so that Watch would chase him.

Suddenly, Benny's foot caught
in a hole and he fell. When he
tried to get up, he couldn't stand
on his right foot. It hurt a lot. So
he just sat down.

"Uh-oh. I hurt my ankle," he said to Watch. "What am I going to do? We need help."

"Help! Help!" Benny shouted. "I'm in the woods!" But there was only silence.

"Watch," Benny said. "Run home and get some help. I'll be all right here."

Benny waited and waited. Finally he heard
a noise. I hope it's not a bear, he thought.

But it wasn't. It was Watch.
And right behind him was Beth.
"What happened to you?" she asked.

Benny said, "I fell."

"That's why Watch was barking so loudly," Beth said.

Benny said proudly, "I told him to get help."

Beth looked at Benny's foot. "It's getting swollen already."

"You'll have to get Henry or Jessie to help me," Benny said.

Beth pulled something out of
her pocket. It was a mushed-up
candy bar. "Here. Keep this, in
case you get hungry." She started
to go, but quickly came back.
She put a water bottle next to him.
"Here. In case you get thirsty."
Then she left.

"Do you think she'll come back?" Benny asked Watch. "I wasn't very nice to her yesterday."

It began to get darker. And cooler. Soon, thunder rumbled in the distance, and Benny felt raindrops on his face. He shivered a little.

Soon he heard Violet's voice.
"Benny, where are you?"
Watch started barking loudly.

When Benny saw Violet and Henry
with Beth, he said, "Wow! Am I glad
to see you!"

Henry had Benny climb on his
back, and they all started home.

The next day, Benny was
playing in his room. He had been
to the doctor. The doctor had
bandaged Benny's ankle.

Benny had his collection of
baseball cards on the floor when
Beth came to the doorway.

"Are you okay?" she asked.

Benny nodded. Then he said, "I'm sure glad I sent Watch for help. A bear might have come."

Beth giggled. "Oh, Benny, there aren't any bears here!"

Beth looked at the cards. "That's a neat collection. You're sure lucky to have it."

Benny said, "I just got some new ones. Do you want to look at them with me?"

Beth said, "That's a great idea! Watch likes them, too."

Girls might not be so bad,
Benny thought.

And now I have a new friend.